CLEARED FOR TAKEOFF

HAVE YOU GOT WHAT IT TAKES TO BE AN AIRLINE PILOT?

by Lisa Thompson

Compass Point Books ✦ Minneapolis, Minnesota

First American edition published in 2009 by
Compass Point Books
151 Good Counsel Drive
P.O. Box 669
Mankato, MN 56002-0669

Editor: Anthony Wacholtz
Designer: Heidi Thompson
Art Director: LuAnn Ascheman-Adams
Creative Director: Joe Ewest
Editorial Director: Nick Healy
Managing Editor: Catherine Neitge
Content Adviser: Jason Wolfe, Captain,
    Delta Airlines

Editor's note: To best explain careers to readers, the author has
created composite characters based on extensive interviews and research.

Copyright © 2008 Blake Publishing Pty Ltd Australia
All rights reserved. No part of this book may be reproduced without
written permission from the publisher. The publisher takes no responsibility
for the use of any of the materials or methods described in this book, nor for
the products thereof.
Printed in the United States of America.

 This book was manufactured with paper containing
at least 10 percent post-consumer waste.

Library of Congress Cataloging-in-Publication Data
Thompson, Lisa.
  Cleared for takeoff : have you got what it takes to be an airline pilot? / by Lisa
Thompson.
      p. cm.—(On the Job)
  Includes index.
  ISBN 978-0-7565-4081-4 (library binding)
 1. Airplanes—Piloting—Vocational Guidance—Juvenile literature.
 2. Aeronautics, Commercial—Vocational guidance—Juvenile literature.
 3. Air pilots—Juvenile literature. I. Title.
    TL561.M67 2009
    629.132'52023—dc22   2008038378

Image Credits: Dan Barnes/iStockphoto, 13 (bottom); Lowell Sannes/Shutterstock,
27 (bottom). All other images are from one of the following royalty-free sources:
Big Stock Photo, Dreamstime, Istock, Photo Objects, Photos.com, and Shutterstock.
Every effort has been made to contact copyright holders of any material reproduced
in this book. Any omission will be rectified in subsequent printings if notice is
given to the publishers.

Visit Compass Point Books on the Internet at *www.compasspointbooks.com*
or e-mail your request to *custserv@compasspointbooks.com*

Contents

Cleared for Takeoff	4
How I Became an Airline Pilot	8
Kinds of Pilots	10
Types of Aircraft	14
The History of Flight	16
Famous Pilots	20
Forces and Flight	22
Aircraft Controls	26
Aircraft Instruments	28
Flight Planning	30
Communication	34
Reading the Weather	36
Black Boxes	38
Preparing to Land	40
Job Opportunities	44
Find out More	46
Glossary	47
Index	48

Cleared for Takeoff

It's 6 A.M., and my alarm goes off. It's time to wake up and make my way from the hotel to the airport.

As a captain working for an international airline, I often stay in hotels overseas. Today I'm flying a Boeing 747 jumbo jet from Bangkok, Thailand, to Sydney, Australia. We're scheduled to leave at 9:30 A.M. I will need to be at the airport by 8:30 A.M. to complete all my preflight checks.

I catch a minibus from the hotel with a group of flight attendants and another pilot. We all work for the same airline. It's a humid, foggy morning in Bangkok, and the traffic is slow. We arrive at the airport just in time.

Bangkok airport

The check-in area is packed as we make our way to the crew area. I meet my first officer, and we go over the flight plan for the journey. We check altitudes and look at predicted weather patterns. We examine the route we are going to take and calculate the fuel needed.

I grab a coffee with the first officer and flight crew before we head to the plane. Once in the cockpit, I check the logbook to see if there were any problems with the plane during its previous flight. I also check the flight controls. When all the passengers have boarded the aircraft, the first officer and I prepare for takeoff.

Loading the luggage

Breakfast in the cockpit

The pilot in command is called the captain. He or she sits on the left side of the cockpit and is in charge of making major decisions, leading the crew team, managing emergencies, and handling troublesome passengers.

The first officer is second in command and sits on the right side of the cockpit. He or she has the same level of training as the captain. Safety is the main reason for having two pilots on a flight. The first officer helps with flying and gives a second opinion on pilot decisions. This reduces the chance of a piloting error occurring.

As we taxi to the runway, the air traffic controller makes contact through my headset. She lets me know the runway is clear. We are ready for takeoff! The first officer takes his foot off the brake pedals, and the plane heads down the runway.

"V1," calls the first officer. This stands for Velocity 1—the speed at which we can still abandon the takeoff if something goes wrong. Within seconds, we are traveling at more than 124 miles (200 kilometers) per hour. "Vr" from the first officer means it's time to pull the control column toward me and rotate the plane. Soon the plane's nose lifts into the air. I pull back a little farther, and the front wheels leave the ground. I pull back even farther, and the plane leaves the ground completely.

"V2," calls the first officer as the plane reaches Velocity 2. This is the speed at which we need to be traveling to climb higher into the air. I pull back on the control column, and the plane soars. As the plane climbs, I bank left to stay on our flight path. At around 33,000 feet (10,000 meters), I push the control column forward to level out the plane. We're on our way to Sydney! It's time to address the passengers: "Good morning everyone. This is captain Gil Morgan speaking."

Tow trucks sometimes help large planes maneuver out of tight spots.

How I Became an Airline Pilot

I've always been fascinated with planes and flying. When I was a child, my grandpa had a farm. He flew a plane to help manage the property, and he took me flying whenever I visited.

A great birthday present

When I turned 16, I got a flying lesson for my birthday. From then on, I was hooked. I read everything I could about planes.

At school, I really liked math and physics. Once I finished school, I went to college to major in aviation. While at college, I was lucky enough to get a job at a local airline hangar. This paid for lots of flying time. I built up my flying hours quickly so that I could get my flying qualification sooner.

A pilot's life

Being an airline pilot is exciting, but it is also hard work. Working hours depend on your destination and flight preparation time. For example, a flight from London to Los Angeles means you will be working very long hours. Sleeping patterns are sometimes irregular, and jet lag may affect your health. Days off depend on the length of your flight. Pilots may also receive free airfares if they want to travel during their time off. Long flights mean time spent away from family and friends.

When I finished college and earned my degree, I found a job with a small courier company. Again, it was all about building up my flying hours. After I had completed enough flying hours, I joined a training program with a domestic commercial airline. I worked there as a pilot for 10 years. I then changed to international flights, or what pilots refer to as long-haul flights.

It is a huge responsibility being captain of a large plane, but flying has never lost its appeal for me. Taking off and landing are still great thrills, even after all these years.

Long-haul flights mean lots of luggage.

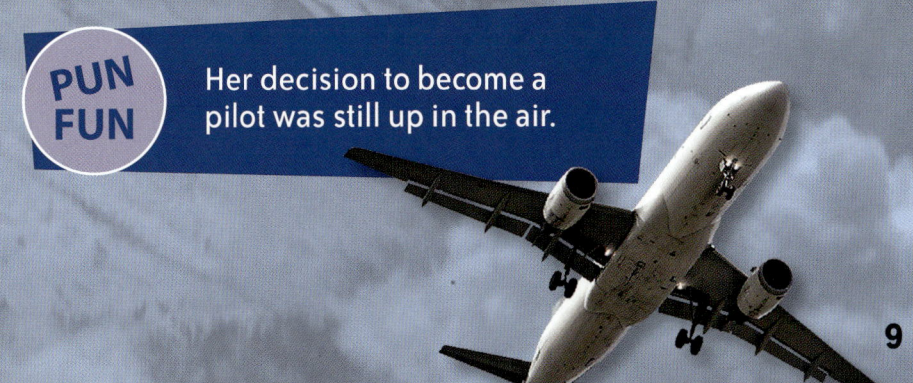

PUN FUN Her decision to become a pilot was still up in the air.

Kinds of Pilots

There are many kinds of pilots. Some pilots fly professionally, and others fly just for fun. Each kind of pilot has a different qualification.

There are four basic types of pilot licenses, from the least to the most qualified:

- student pilot license
- private pilot license
- commercial pilot license (CPL)
- air transport pilot license (ATPL)

CPL vs. ATPL
You need a CPL to earn an income from flying an aircraft. With a CPL, you can fly charters, scenic flights, and low-capacity airlines. You need an ATPL to be a captain on an aircraft that requires two pilots, or any other multi-crew aircraft.

Pilot stripes

The number of stripes on the sleeves of uniform jackets and on the shoulders of a uniform shirt indicate the following ranks:
4 stripes—captain
3 stripes—first officer
2 stripes—second officer

Pilots can also train for additional qualifications:
- flying special types of aircraft, such as seaplanes
- instrument rating, such as flying in clouds or at night
- certified flight instruction (teaching others to fly)
- aerobatic flying, such as learning to do loop-the-loops

Good eye
To qualify for a commercial pilot license or to join a military pilot training program, your eyesight must be excellent. Also, you cannot be color-blind.

In the military

People learn to fly through the military as well, but their licensing system differs from the civilian one. The Air Force, Army, and Navy all control aircraft equipped with some kind of firepower.

Student pilot

This is where all pilots start. The training varies depending on the type of license the pilot is trying to get. While training, flying privileges are limited. Students are introduced to the basics of flying, such as interaction with air traffic control and airport-to-airport and cross-country flying skills.

Approaching the runway

Student pilots must complete all their flights with a flight instructor on board. A student pilot can only fly solo once they:

- are over the age of 16
- have passed medical testing
- have mastered the basic skills and topics of flight
- have received their instructor's sign-off

Private pilots

Private pilots are the largest group of pilots. They must be at least 17 years of age and have a minimum of 40 hours of flight experience. This includes:

- five hours of general flight time as the pilot in command
- five hours of cross-country flight time as the pilot in command
- two hours of instrument flight time

A private jet aircraft

Private pilots are not paid to fly, but are allowed to share the flight's operating expenses with their passengers.

The interior of a luxury private jet

Commercial pilots

Commercial pilots are paid to fly aircraft. In the United States, they must be at least 18 years of age and have from 200 to 250 hours of flying experience. The flying experience includes:

- 100 hours of general flight time as the pilot in command
- 50 hours of cross-country as the pilot in command
- 10 hours of instrument training

Types of Aircraft

There are many kinds of aircraft, such as microlights, helicopters, light aircraft, and military aircraft. Airplanes carry passengers, freight, and sometimes weapons.

Jumbo jets
Jumbo jets like the Boeing 747 can fly long distances. They hold about 400 passengers and fly all around the world.

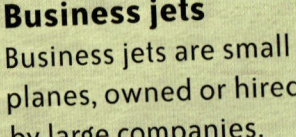

Light aircraft
Light aircraft are small planes, usually with a single engine. Some can carry three or four passengers. Light aircraft can take off and land in small airfields.

Business jets
Business jets are small planes, owned or hired by large companies.

Seaplanes
Seaplanes are fitted with special floats so they can land on water.

Cargo carriers
Cargo carriers transport goods to all parts of the world. With some carriers, the tail can swing aside or the nose can swing open for easy loading.

Military aircraft
Military transport planes carry weapons, large numbers of troops, and equipment such as tanks and trucks. Air-combat planes carry out attacks or reconnaissance missions.

Microlights
Microlights are simple planes. They are similar to hang gliders with a small engine attached, and they can carry one or two people.

Hot air balloons
Commercial hot air balloon pilots must have a commercial pilot license.

The History of Flight

More than 700 years ago, the Chinese invented the first kites. This started humans thinking about flying. Kites are important to the history of flight because they were the forerunner to balloons and gliders.

Chinese kite c. 1800

Ideas take flight

A statue of Leonardo da Vinci in Florence, Italy

More than 500 years ago, the Italian artist and inventor Leonardo da Vinci drew designs for flying machines. His ornithopter flying machine demonstrated how man could fly. The modern-day helicopter is based on this concept. His theories about flight were correct, but at the time there wasn't an engine powerful enough to make his machines work.

In the 1880s, the gasoline engine was invented. This made it possible to fly aircraft powered by an engine. In 1903, the Wright brothers, Wilbur and Orville, made the world's first powered, controlled, and sustained flight in the aircraft *Flyer 1*. Orville Wright flew the plane for 199 feet (36 m), about 10 feet (3 m) off the ground. Later that day, Wilbur Wright flew for 59 seconds.

Wilbur Wright and **Flyer 1**

After they made improvements to the aircraft, the Wright brothers flew for about an hour. Within six years, pilots in the United States and France began using the Wrights' aircraft designs.

The Wright brothers' airplane, Flyer 1, is in the National Air and Space Museum in Washington, D.C.

Flight Timeline

Airplanes have changed a lot since they were invented!

1937—The jet engine is built by British engineer Frank Whittle

1939—Russian-American engineer Igor Sikorsky designs the first successful helicopter

1947—The first aircraft flies at supersonic speed in the United States

1949—The De Havilland Comet, the first commercial airliner, enters service in the United Kingdom

1970—The Boeing 747 jumbo jet is launched

Many modern fighter jets are supersonic.

1976—The world's first supersonic commercial airliner, the Concorde, makes its first scheduled flight from London to Washington, D.C.

2006—The largest commercial aircraft, the Airbus A380, makes its first commercial flight from Singapore to Sydney

Nicknamed the Super Jumbo, the Airbus A380 is the length of eight buses and has enough room on its massive wings to park 70 cars.

2009—Virgin Galactic plans the world's first commercial flights into space

A380 vs. 747

The Airbus A380 is currently the largest commercial airliner in the world. It is 50 feet (15 m) wider, 13 feet (4 m) taller, 6½ feet (2 m) longer, and 130 tons (118 metric tons) heavier than the Boeing 747. The A380 has space for cocktail bars, billiard rooms, showers, libraries, and sleeping quarters tucked under the floorboards for staff. However, with a 263-foot (79.8-m) wingspan, it is too large for most airport docking bays.

Famous Pilots

Louis Bleriot
The Frenchman Louis Bleriot designed and built a series of planes. In 1909, he became the first person to fly across the English Channel. He flew 22 miles (35 km) in 37 minutes. Bleriot reported that he had to wrestle the controls constantly to keep his monoplane steady.

Charles Lindbergh
In 1927, American Charles Lindbergh was the first person to fly solo, nonstop across the Atlantic Ocean. It took him 33 hours and 39 minutes to fly 3,596 miles (5,789 km) from New York to Paris in his monoplane *Spirit of St. Louis*. His average speed for the flight was 107 miles (172 km) per hour.

Charles Kingford Smith and Charles Ulm

Charles Kingsford Smith and his co-pilot, Charles Ulm, were famous Australian pilots who set many flying records. In 1928, they became the first pilots to fly across the Pacific Ocean. Their flight from San Francisco to Brisbane took nine and a half days. Kingford disappeared over Calcutta, India, during a flight in 1935.

Amelia Earhart

Amelia Earhart was an American pilot who became famous for her daring, long-distance flights. In 1932, flying her Lockheed Vega plane, she became the first woman to fly solo across the Atlantic Ocean. In 1935, she was the first woman to fly from Hawaii to California. Earhart disappeared over the Pacific Ocean during a 1937 flight and was never found.

Forces and Flight

When an aircraft becomes airborne, there are four forces at work: thrust, weight, drag, and lift. Airplanes need engine power to provide thrust, pushing the aircraft forward. Friction against the rushing air produces drag.

Drag slows the movement of the aircraft. Lift from under the wings holds the airplane up, and the weight of the airplane pulls it down. When an airplane is in the air and all four forces are in balance, the aircraft flies straight and at a steady speed.

Up, up, and away!

You need a lot of lift to keep an 875,000-pound (393,750-kg) Boeing 747 jumbo in the air. That's why it has such massive wings. The total area of a 747's wings is 630 square yards (529 square meters). That's big enough to fit about 45 cars!

PUN FUN — A young pilot was taking a flying test in an airplane and flew through a rainbow. He passed with flying colors.

An airplane's wings have an airfoil shape. This means the top surface of the wing is more curved than the lower surface. The airfoil shape means that air flows faster above the wing than below it. The faster moving air sucks the wing upward, creating an upward force called lift.

Bernoulli's principle

Airplanes fly using Bernoulli's principle. The faster an airplane's wings move through the air, the more pressure and lift is created. As air flows over the curved top of an airplane's wing, it must flow faster, and its pressure is lowered. The air flowing underneath the wing has to travel a shorter distance, allowing it to also travel at a slower speed. This creates higher pressure beneath the wing, causing the wing to be pushed upward.

Control Surfaces

Control surfaces are the moving parts of the aircraft. They make the plane climb, descend, and turn in flight.

There are three main control surfaces:

1. The rudder on the tail fin moves the plane's nose left or right and keeps the plane balanced.
2. Elevators on the tail lift the nose up or down.
3. Ailerons on the wings control the direction of the roll or bank of the plane.

Winglets

Elevators

Pilots change the shape of the wings during takeoff and landing to control lift. Increasing the size of the wing increases lift, and flying at a lower speed reduces lift. This makes it possible for the aircraft to descend. Modern commercial aircraft have winglets. They help reduce drag and improve fuel efficiency.

The pilot moves the panels to control the plane's movement.

Pilots change the wing shape using ailerons and spoilers. Ailerons give the aircraft roll control. *Aileron* is a French word that means "little wing." They are hinged surfaces on the outer edge of aircraft wings. Unlike spoilers, ailerons are always used at the same time so that when one goes up, the other goes down.

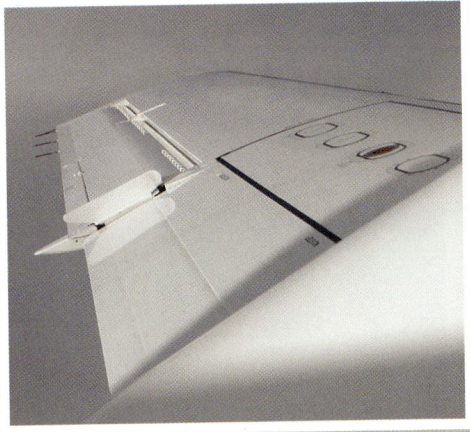

Spoilers

Spoilerons are wing panels that assist in roll control. Spoilers, on the other hand, are installed on the top surface of the wing and reduce lift. There are two types of spoilers: flight and ground. They "spoil" the lifting ability of the wing. Flight spoilers are used in the air, and ground spoilers are used once the wheels touch land, helping the plane stay on the ground.

25

Aircraft Controls

There are a number of standard controls found in an aircraft.

Throttle
The throttle adjusts the thrust that the engines produce.

Control column
The control column controls the steering of the aircraft. It is connected to ailerons on the wings and elevator panels on the tail. Pilots use the column to control climbing, diving, and banking left or right.

Rudder pedals
Rudder pedals control the rudder. The rudder balances the aircraft while turning or when strong winds move the aircraft.

Brakes
Brakes stop the aircraft and control how it turns once it is on the ground. Aircraft may also have a parking brake to stop it from rolling when parked.

Spoiler levers
They control the spoilers on the wings, especially when landing.

Flap levers
They control the wings' flaps.

Spoiler levers control panels on the wings.

Trim controls
They are usually knobs that adjust pitch or roll.

Autopilot
Large, complex aircraft have autopilot controls. The autopilot system is part of an aircraft's electronic equipment. Autopilot controls are used to maintain altitude, climb, descend, or turn—anything that a human pilot can do. They are very useful on long flights—they allow pilots to take a break.

The magnetic compass

The magnetic compass links all forms of aeronautical navigation. Almost every type of plane has a simple magnetic compass mounted to the windshield of the instrument panel. It is extremely reliable, and it doesn't use power or advanced technology. Every airway and runway is numbered according to its magnetic or compass orientation.

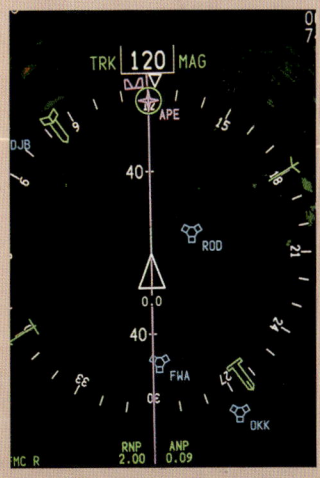

Aircraft Instruments

Modern aircraft have instruments to provide the pilot with important information. Basic aircraft instruments include:

Modern airplanes have many instruments to watch.

- **airspeed indicator**—indicates how fast the plane is moving through the air
- **altimeter**—indicates the altitude of the aircraft, above the ground or above sea level
- **attitude indicator**—also called an artificial horizon, indicates the exact orientation of the plane as it pitches and rolls through the air

Most aircraft also have these instruments:

- **turn coordinator**—helps the pilot to maintain control while turning the aircraft
- **rate-of-climb indicator**—shows the rate at which the aircraft is climbing or descending
- **engine instruments**—show the status of each aircraft engine, including the operating speed, thrust, oil temperature, and oil pressure
- **navigation and flight plan displays**—help pilots stay on course
- **weather radar displays**—indicate oncoming weather conditions

Navigation instruments

Navigation instruments help aircraft fly in and above the clouds without any visual points of reference.

Planes follow set routes from airport to airport. Radio signals from beacons, which are hundreds of miles apart, identify these routes. Each beacon has its own signal, and airplanes tune into the signal, similar to tuning into a radio station.

Until recently, pilots used a radio magnetic indicator to navigate. Today there are inertial reference systems and global positioning systems to help aircraft fly more efficient, direct routes. The inertial reference systems are onboard gyroscopes that determine the aircraft's position as it flies.

Flight Planning

Planning a flight involves two important safety aspects:

1. Calculating the amount of fuel the airplane needs to reach its destination.

2. Ensuring a safe route to avoid collision with buildings, trees, mountains, or other airplanes.

It's helpful knowing ahead of time what you'll be flying into.

Flight planning depends on accurate weather forecasts. Strong headwinds and tailwinds and changes in air temperature affect how much fuel a plane consumes. Safety regulations require planes to carry more than the minimum amount of fuel needed. A pilot sends the flight plan to the control tower around 30 minutes before departure.

Flight management systems
Modern commercial aircraft use internal flight-management systems. These computer systems monitor information such as flight routes, aircraft speed, engine settings, and estimated times of arrival. They update the aircraft's flight plan throughout the flight.

Air traffic control towers

A commercial flight plan includes:
- the airline name and flight number
- the type of aircraft and equipment
- the intended airspeed and cruising altitude
- the route of flight, including the departure and destination airports

A flight plan usually has an alternative destination airport in case of unforeseen circumstances such as bad weather.

PUN FUN — If you step onto a plane and recognize your friend Jack, don't yell out, "Hi Jack!"

Once the air traffic controllers in the control tower have the flight-plan information, they generate a flight progress report from a computer. This will pass from controller to controller throughout the plane's flight. The report is constantly updated and contains all the necessary data to track the plane during its flight.

U-turn in a plane

Planes do not turn—they bank, or lean, in the direction the pilot steers. For example, to bank left, the pilot moves the control column left. This makes the ailerons on the left wing tilt up, pushing the wing down. The ailerons on the right wing tilt down, pushing the wing up.

Planes follow routes called airways. They are like a plane's personal road. They prevent mid-flight collisions. Airways are separated vertically by 1,000 feet to 2,000 feet (305 m to 610 m).

Most commercial planes travel between airports. Private aircraft, commercial sightseeing tours, and military planes may land at the same airport from which they took off. These are known as circular or out-and-back flights.

Faster than sound

The Concorde was the only commercial aircraft faster than the speed of sound. It stopped flying in 2003 because of safety concerns.

Communication

Pilots use special code words to communicate with fellow pilots and control towers. The North Atlantic Treaty Organization (NATO) phonetic alphabet assigns code words to the letters of the English alphabet. Correct pronunciation of the words over radio or telephone is important.

The NATO Phonetic Alphabet

LETTER	CODE WORD	PRONUNCIATION
A	Alpha	AL-FAH
B	Bravo	BRAH-VOH
C	Charlie	CHAR-LEE
D	Delta	DELL-TAH
E	Echo	ECK-OH
F	Foxtrot	FOKS-TROT
G	Golf	GOLF
H	Hotel	HO-TELL
I	India	IN-DEE-AH
J	Juliet	JEW-LEE-ETT
K	Kilo	KEY-LOH
L	Lima	LEE-MAH
M	Mike	MIKE
N	November	NOH-VEM-BER
O	Oscar	OSS-CAH
P	Papa	PAH-PAH
Q	Quebec	KEH-BECK
R	Romeo	ROW-ME-OH
S	Sierra	SEE-AIR-RAH
T	Tango	TANG-GO
U	Uniform	YOU-NEE-FORM
V	Victor	VIK-TAH
W	Whiskey	WISS-KEY
X	X-ray	EX-RAY
Y	Yankee	YANK-KEY
Z	Zulu	ZOO-LOO

Call signs

International aircraft have a registration number, just like a car. It is made up of a country prefix and a series of letters and numbers. For example, a plane registered as N9876T would use this call sign: November, niner, eight, seven, six, tango.

Learn the lingo

PILOT SPEAK	MEANING
Affirmative	Yes
Negative	No
Mayday Emergency	Help
Roger Message	Message received
ETA	Estimated time of arrival
ETD	Estimated time of departure

Reading the Weather

Pilots must constantly keep an eye on weather conditions. Weather radar in a plane's nose beams radio signals at clouds. The signals bounce back and let the pilot know how big and close the clouds are.

Turbulence

Storm clouds also appear on a plane's navigation display. Rough conditions inside clouds are called turbulence. Turbulence occurs when there are gusty, unpredictable air currents. It often occurs unexpectedly.

PUN FUN Airline pilots make many friends in high places.

Fear of flying

Fliers overestimate the effects of turbulence. What passengers might consider a bumpy ride will only appear as a slight jiggle on the cockpit altimeter. Pilots avoid unstable air if possible so their passengers feel more comfortable. But weather reports aren't always reliable. Most of the time, the pilot and crew know that all they can do is sit back and wait for the gusty winds to pass.

A number of weather conditions cause turbulence. The most common is a thunderstorm. Flying through a patch of clouds will often jostle the aircraft. Turbulence is also caused by flying over mountains, near jet streams at high altitude, near a frontal system, or where there are temperature changes in the air.

Turbulence may also occur when the sky is clear of clouds. This is called clear-air turbulence. CAT occurs when a plane flies from a slow-moving air mass of about 12 to 23 miles (19 to 37 km) per hour or near a jet stream moving at more than 115 miles (185 km) per hour. CAT doesn't appear on the radar, but flight-plan forecasts warn pilots of possible turbulence ahead.

Black Boxes

If a plane crashes, it's important to find out what went wrong. Planes carry a device called a black box that contains a flight-data recorder and a cockpit voice recorder. They record vital information on a plane prior to an accident. Black boxes are built to withstand extreme heat, violent crashes, and enormous amounts of pressure. They are often the only devices left intact after an airline accident. Black boxes provide investigators with clues as to why a plane crashed.

Black boxes contain the following data:
- time
- altitude
- air pressure
- air speed
- vertical acceleration
- magnetic heading
- control column position
- rudder pedal position
- control wheel position
- fuel flow
- horizontal stabilizer
- temperature

Black boxes record both the cabin temperature and the outside temperature.

Planes are fitted with sensors that gather data. These sensors monitor acceleration, airspeed, altitude, wing-flap settings, outside temperature, cabin temperature and pressure, and engine performance. All the sensor data are collected and eventually sent to the black boxes.

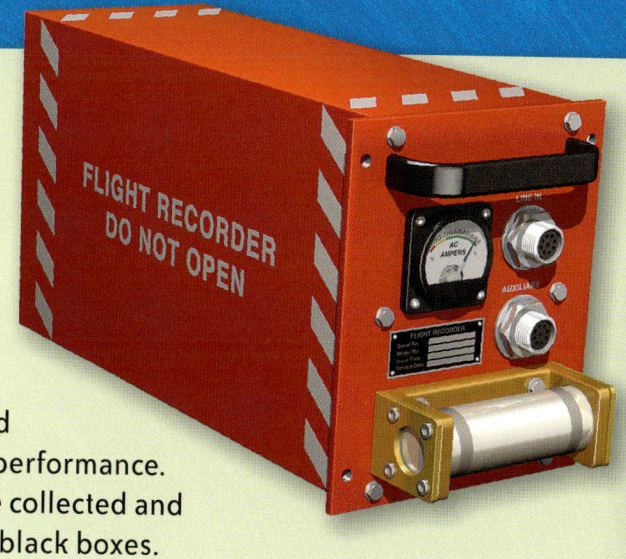

Cockpit voice recorders
Microphones in the plane's cockpit record conversations of the flight crew. They also pick up any background noises in the cockpit, such as knocks or thuds.

Preparing to Land

As we fly out of the storm cloud, I contact Sydney air traffic control. They let me know bad weather has delayed our landing time. I need to circle the airport while we wait for the bad weather to pass.

I alert the crew and the passengers of the delay. If the weather doesn't clear, air traffic control may ask us to land at a different airport. We have enough fuel—but they need to let us know soon.

After about 10 minutes, they give us the all-clear to land. It is once again time to address the passengers: "Ladies and gentlemen, we are about to begin our descent."

Passengers may have to wait patiently if the plane has to go into a holding pattern.

PUN FUN
When you're wearing a watch on an airplane, time flies.

I push the control column forward. The altimeter indicator shows I am flying at the height requested by air traffic control. I then pull back on the column to level out the plane. Adjusting the wing spoilers to reduce the lift, we continue our descent and approach the runway.

Around five miles (eight kilometers) from the airport, the primary flight display picks up two signals from the runway. These signals help guide us onto the runway. One of them gives me the correct angle of our descent. The other helps the pilot keep the plane in line with the center of the runway.

The runway lights guide the pilot in for a safe landing.

Pink beams

An airport's landing beams make a pink cross appear on the primary flight display's artificial horizon. Using the control column, the pilot lines the white bars up with the pink cross to make the plane stay on course.

Touchdown

I slow the plane's speed and pull the wing-flap lever down. This increases the wings' edges so we can fly at a slower speed. The runway rushes toward us. The first officer pulls a lever to lower the plane's wheels.

I pull the control column back, and the plane's nose tips up. I reduce the engine power, and the plane touches down on the runway.

I put the engines into reverse, slowing down our forward movement. Now instead of thrust coming out of the back of the engine, it shoots forward out of the vents. At the same time, the wheel brakes come on, and we gently roll to a stop. We then steer the plane toward our designated arrival gate.

Chocs away

When a plane has come to a halt, blocks called chocs are put in front of the wheels. They stop the plane from rolling away. The chocs must be removed before the plane can take off.

I address the passengers, "This is your captain speaking. Welcome to Sydney. I trust you all had a pleasant flight, and I hope we will fly together again soon."

The ground crew directs us into our parking spot.

Traffic jam on the runway—luckily I'm not flying out again tonight.

Follow These Steps to Become a Commercial Pilot

People who want to become a pilot have a few options.

Option 1

Step 1 Finish high school with the best grades possible in all subjects, particularly mathematics, physics, and geography.

Step 2 Continue your education at a college or university. Some colleges offer specific commercial pilot training courses. A degree, such as a bachelor's degree in aviation, will provide you with the skills and training you need.

Step 3 Undertake specific ongoing training for aviation ratings and licenses. The amount of study you do will depend on the level of qualifications you want to pursue.

Step 4 Pass all medical tests.

Step 5 Understand that becoming a pilot takes dedication and patience. A pilot's seniority depends on his or her length of service.

In addition to major airline companies, commercial pilots can also find employment with:

- government agencies, such as the police, customs, U.S. Coast Guard, and forest and national parks
- aerial surveying services, such as aerial photography and civil engineering projects
- aeromedical services, such as services that fly doctors and/or nurses to remote areas where people need medical care
- aircraft sales companies

Option 2

Step 1 Complete a course at a flight training school.

Step 2 Get as many flying hours as are required to gain a commercial pilot license.

Step 3 Pass all medical checks, tests, and examinations required for specific qualifications.

Step 4 Get as much flying experience as possible with all types of aircraft.

Option 3

Step 1 Finish college.

Step 2 Apply to be a military pilot.

Commercial pilots must also:
- pass a medical examination by a doctor
- have good eyesight, though you can wear glasses, if needed
- make accurate judgments quickly and remain calm in an emergency
- be able to use information from various sources and make sound decisions quickly
- speak, write, and understand English

Find Out More

In the Know

- Pilots use a personal checklist before takeoff to make sure they're physically and mentally safe to fly and are not impaired by Illness, Medication, Stress, Alcohol, Fatigue, Emotion (I'M SAFE).
- In 2005, a Boeing 777 jet flew 11,664 nautical miles (21,601 km), setting a world record for a nonstop distance traveled by a commercial airplane. The record beat the previous record set in 1989 by more than 2,400 nautical miles (4,422 km).
- In 1929, there were 9,215 holders of pilot certificates. By 2007, the number increased to more than 624,000.
- As of May 2007, the U.S. Department of Labor estimates that the average salary for a commercial pilot is $71,270. The lowest 10 percent earned $30,460, and the highest 10 percent earned more than $122,550.

Further Reading

Fleischman, John. *Black and White Airmen: Their True History*. Boston: Houghton Mifflin, 2007.

Nahum, Andrew. *Flying Machine*. New York: DK Publishing, 2004.

Rauf, Don, and Monique Vescia. *Airline Pilot*. New York: Ferguson Publishing, 2008.

Rinard, Judith E. *Book of Flight*. Buffalo, N.Y.: Firefly Books, 2007.

On the Web

For more information on this topic, use FactHound.
1. Go to *www.facthound.com*
2. Choose your grade level.
3. Begin your search.
This book's ID number is 9780756540814
FactHound will find the best sites for you.

Glossary

aeronautical—relating to aircraft or their flight

airfoil—shape of an airplane's wing that creates lift

aviation—field that deals with the design, manufacture, and use of aircraft

bank—to angle an airplane so it leans, making it turn in the desired direction

beacon—radio transmitter that broadcasts a signal to guide aircraft

civil engineering—field of study dealing with designing and building roads and bridges

domestic—occurring within a country

drag—force created by friction that slows down the airplane

frontal system—where one mass of air meets another that is different in temperature or density

gyroscope—rotating heavy metal wheel inside a circular frame that lets the wheel's axis keep its original direction even though the frame is moved around; used in compasses and other navigational aids

hangar—large building where aircraft are kept or repaired

jet lag—feeling people get after traveling through several time zones; often causes fatigue

jet stream—strong high-altitude wind current

lift—upward force

monoplane—airplane that has just one pair of wings

navigate—to figure out the direction you should travel, sometimes using maps or instruments

pitch—to move in a rolling front-to-rear motion

supersonic—moving faster than the speed of sound

thrust—force created by the engines that moves the airplane forward

Index

ailerons, 24, 25, 26, 32
Airbus A380 aircraft, 19
aircraft controls, 5, 7, 20, 26–27, 32, 38, 41, 42
airports, 4, 12, 19, 29, 31, 33, 40, 41
airspeed indicators, 28
air traffic control, 12, 30, 32, 40, 41
air transport pilot licenses, 10
airways, 27, 33
altimeters, 28, 37, 41
altitude, 5, 27, 28, 31, 37, 38, 39
autopilot controls, 27

banking, 7, 24, 26, 32
Bernoulli's principle, 23
black boxes, 38, 39
Bleriot, Louis, 20
Boeing 747 jumbo jets, 4, 14, 18, 22
brakes, 6, 26, 42

call signs, 35
chocs, 42
clear-air turbulence (CAT), 37
cockpit voice recorders, 38, 39
commercial pilot licenses, 10, 11, 15, 45
Concorde airliner, 19, 33
control column, 7, 26, 32, 38, 41, 42
control surfaces, 24–25

De Havilland Comet airliner, 18
drag, 22, 25

Earhart, Amelia, 21
education, 8, 9, 11, 44, 45
elevator panels, 24, 26
engines, 14, 15, 16, 17, 18, 22, 26, 29, 30, 39, 42
eyesight, 11, 45

flap levers, 27
flight crews, 5, 6, 10, 37, 39, 40
flight management systems, 30
flight plans, 5, 30, 31, 32
flight progress reports, 32
Flyer 1 (aircraft), 17
fuel, 5, 25, 30, 38, 40

global positioning systems, 29

history, 16–17, 18–19, 20–21

inertial reference systems, 29
instruments, 11, 12, 13, 28–29

jets, 4, 14, 18

landings, 9, 25, 27, 40–41, 42
licensing, 10, 11, 12, 15, 44, 45
lift, 22, 23, 25, 41
Lindbergh, Charles, 20
Lockheed Vega aircraft, 21

magnetic compasses, 27
military, 11, 14, 15, 33, 45

navigation instruments, 27, 29, 36
North Atlantic Treaty Organization (NATO), 34
nose, 7, 15, 24, 36, 42

passengers, 5, 6, 7, 13, 14, 37, 40, 43
phonetic alphabet, 34
pitch, 27, 28
pressure, 23, 38, 39
private pilots, 10, 12–13

qualifications, 8, 10–11, 45

radar, 29, 36, 37
ranks, 10
rate-of-climb indicators, 29
registration numbers, 35
roll, 24, 25, 27, 28
rudders, 24, 26, 38
runways, 6, 27, 41, 42

safety, 6, 30, 33
sensors, 39
Sikorsky, Igor, 18
Smith, Charles Kingford, 21
speed, 7, 18, 20, 22, 23, 25, 28, 29, 30, 31, 33, 38, 39, 42
Spirit of St. Louis (monoplane), 20
spoilers, 25, 27, 41
steering, 26, 32, 42
student pilots, 10, 12

takeoffs, 5, 6–7, 9, 25
throttle, 26
thrust, 22, 26, 29, 42
trim controls, 27
turbulence, 36, 37
turn coordinators, 29
turns. *See* banking.

Ulm, Charles, 21

Vinci, Leonardo da, 16
Virgin Galactic space flights, 19

weather, 5, 29, 30, 31, 36, 37, 40
wheels, 7, 25, 42
Whittle, Frank, 18
winglets, 25
wings, 19, 22, 23, 24, 25, 26, 27, 32, 39, 42
Wright brothers, 17

Look for More Books in This Series:

Battling Blazes: Have You Got What It Takes to Be a Firefighter?

Cover Story: Have You Got What It Takes to Be a Magazine Editor?

Eyes for Evidence: Have You Got What It Takes to Be a Forensic Scientist?

Going Live in 3, 2, 1: Have You Got What It Takes to Be a TV Producer?

Hard Hat Area: Have You Got What It Takes to Be a Contractor?

Pop the Hood: Have You Got What It Takes to Be an Auto Technician?

Sea Life Scientist: Have You Got What It Takes to Be a Marine Biologist?

Trauma Shift: Have You Got What It Takes to Be an ER Nurse?

Wild About Wildlife: Have You Got What It Takes to Be a Zookeeper?

SAYVILLE LIBRARY
88 GREENE AVENUE
SAYVILLE, NY 11782

NOV 1 9 2009

**DISCARDED BY
SAYVILLE LIBRARY**